# Billie B. Brown

www.BillieBBrownBooks.com

# *Billie B. Brown* Books

The Bad Butterfly
The Soccer Star
The Midnight Feast
The Second-best Friend
The Extra-special Helper
The Beautiful Haircut
The Big Sister
The Spotty Vacation
The Birthday Mix-up
The Secret Message
The Little Lie
The Best Project
The Deep End
The Copycat Kid
The Night Fright
The Bully Buster
The Missing Tooth
The Book Buddies

First American Edition 2020
Kane Miller, A Division of EDC Publishing
Original Title: Billie B. Brown: The Missing Tooth
Text Copyright © 2012 Sally Rippin
Illustration Copyright © 2012 Aki Fukuoka
Logo and Design Copyright © 2012 Hardie Grant Egmont
First published in Australia by Hardie Grant Egmont

For information contact:
Kane Miller, A Division of EDC Publishing
P.O. Box 470663
Tulsa, OK 74147-0663
**www.kanemiller.com**
**www.edcpub.com**
**www.usbornebooksandmore.com**

Library of Congress Control Number: 2019951180

Printed and bound in the United States of America
3 4 5 6 7 8 9 10
ISBN: 978-1-68464-131-4

# Billie B. Brown

# The Missing Tooth

By Sally Rippin

Illustrated by Aki Fukuoka

**Kane Miller**
A DIVISION OF EDC PUBLISHING

# Chapter One

Billie B. Brown has two messy pigtails, fifteen freckles and one wobbly tooth. Do you know what the "B" in Billie B. Brown stands for?

# Bother.

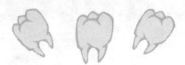

Every morning this week, Billie B. Brown has stood in front of the mirror and wiggled and jiggled her wobbly tooth. But it is no use. The tooth is stuck. What a bother!

Fifteen freckles

Two messy pigtails

One wobbly tooth

"Billie, stop fiddling with your tooth," Billie's mom says. "It will come out when it's ready. Hurry and brush your teeth or you'll be late for school."

Billie's mom is a bit **grumpy** today. Noah has been crying a lot in the night, so she is very tired.

4

Noah's cheeks are bright red and he is very **dribbly**. Billie's mom says he is teething.

Billie brushes her teeth carefully. Billie's dad pokes his head into the bathroom.

"I can pull out your tooth for you," he jokes.

6

"I just have to tie one end of a string around your tooth and the other end to the doorknob. Then, **slam!** Out pops the tooth!"

"No way!" says Billie, spitting toothpaste into the sink. "That will hurt!"

Billie walks to school with her dad and her best friend, Jack.

On the way, she starts wiggling the wobbly tooth again.

"How about eating an apple?" Jack suggests. "That's how I lost one of mine."

Billie shakes her head. "That might hurt," she says.

She pushes her hands
down into her pockets
to stop her fingers from
creeping up to her mouth.

At school, Billie's class is learning about teeth. They learn that an elephant has big pointy teeth called tusks. Crocodiles have seventy teeth and sharks have three sets of teeth. Even slugs have teeth!

Ms. Walton asks how many people in the class have lost a tooth.

Everyone puts up their hand – except Billie.

Billie frowns and looks down at her desk.

*Hurry up, tooth!* she thinks.

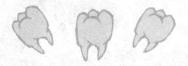

# Chapter Two

At recess, Billie and
Jack play tag with some
other kids in their class.
First Jack is "it." He
chases Billie around the
playground.

Billie is very fast, but Jack traps her near the water fountain. "Billie's 'it'!" he shouts.

Billie decides she is going to catch Mika next. Mika

is a fast runner too. But not as fast as Billie. Billie runs and runs and runs and…Oh no! Billie trips. She falls down hard onto the concrete.

Even though she stuck out her hands, Billie still bangs her chin on the ground. She sits up and **howls**.

Billie's hands are grazed,
her knees are grazed –
even her chin is grazed.
She feels **sore** all over.
Poor Billie!

Jack rushes over.
Mika, Ella and Tracey
rush over too. Hot tears
stream down Billie's cheeks.
Mika puts her arm
around Billie.

"I'll take her to the nurse!" Ella offers.

"No, I will!" says Tracey. "It's my turn."

"You can all come," Billie sniffles. "I need all of you to help me walk. My knees hurt SO much."

Billie's friends help her stand up.

"Wait!" Jack says. "Look!"

Billie looks at the ground. There, in the dust, is something very small and white. It's not much bigger than a grain of rice. Can you guess what it is?

"My tooth!" Billie **gasps**.

Billie slips her tongue into the gap between her teeth.

It feels **squishy** and tastes like metal. Billie knows that taste. She gasps again. "Is there blood?"

Ella peers into Billie's mouth. "A little bit," she says.

Tracey scrunches up her face like she has swallowed something sour.

Billie begins to feel **worried**.

"It's fine," says Jack. "There's hardly any." He picks up the tiny tooth and hands it to Billie.

Just then Ms. Walton
walks over.

"Billie fell down!" Ella
shouts.

"Oh my goodness," says
Ms. Walton. "Look at
your poor knees. And
your chin! We'd better
get you cleaned up."

"Look!" Billie says.
She shows Ms. Walton the
little tooth in her hand.

Ms. Walton smiles.
She pulls out a tissue
from her pocket. "Here,"

she says. "You don't want to lose that. Wrap it up so you can take it home for the Tooth Fairy."

Billie grins. The Tooth Fairy! Even though her knees and hands and chin hurt, she can't help feeling **excited**.

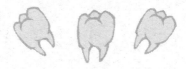

# Chapter Three

Billie's dad picks her
up after school. Billie is
covered in bandages.

"Oh no, Billie! What
happened?" her dad asks.

But Billie is too excited
to bother about all
her injuries.

"I fell down. But look!"
Billie says. Carefully she
unwraps the tissue to
show her dad the tooth.

Billie's dad smiles.
"How exciting," he says.
"Don't lose it, will you?
Looks like the Tooth
Fairy might be visiting
our house tonight!"

Billie gives a **happy**
little squeal. She wraps
the tooth up in the
tissue again and puts
it in her pocket.

All the way home in
the car, her tongue keeps
wriggling into the empty
space in her mouth.

When they get home,
Billie runs into the house
to show her mom her
tooth. Billie's mom is on
the couch feeding Noah.
She looks very tired.

"Mom, Mom!" Billie yells. "Look, look!"

Billie yells so **loudly** that Noah gets a fright and starts crying. At first Billie's mom looks cross.

But then she sees all Billie's bandages. "Oh, my poor little soldier! What happened to you?" she says.

"I fell down," Billie says glumly. "But look!" She opens her mouth to show the gap where her tooth had once been.

"Your tooth came out!" says Billie's mom.

She gives Billie a cuddle. Noah grizzles unhappily.

Billie frowns. "He's always crying these days," she says **crossly**.

Billie's mom stands up to rock Noah to sleep.

"It's not his fault," she sighs. "He is growing teeth, Billie. They hurt his gums."

But Billie doesn't want to talk about Noah's teeth. She wants to talk about hers! "Look," Billie says. She reaches into her pocket and pulls out the tissue.

She opens it up carefully,
but…the tissue is empty!

"Wait," says Billie.
She checks her pocket.
There is nothing there.

"Oh no," she says. She feels
her bottom lip begin to
tremble. "I can't find it!"

"Maybe it fell out in
the car?" Billie's mom says.

Billie checks the car
all over. But the tooth is
nowhere to be found.

Billie starts to cry. Her knees
hurt, her hands hurt, even
her chin hurts. And now
she has lost her tooth, too!

# Chapter Four

That night, Billie's dad tucks Noah into bed. Her mom sits on Billie's bed. Billie still feels very **upset**.

"Oh, Billie," says her mom.

She gives Billie a cuddle.
"Maybe the Tooth Fairy
will still come?"

But Billie shakes her
head sadly. It's no use.
Everyone knows the
Tooth Fairy only comes if
there is a tooth to collect.

Just then Billie has an idea.

A super-duper idea.

"I know!" she says, wiping
her eyes. "Maybe I can write
the Tooth Fairy a note?"

"That's a great idea!" says
Billie's mom.

So Billie gets out her
sparkly pens and writes
a note for the fairy.
She even draws a picture.

Dear Tooth Fairy,

I lost my first tooth today.
I fell down at school and
banged my chin and my tooth
came out. But then I lost
my tooth on my way home from school (this is the truth!).
Can you please still leave me some money anyway?
Otherwise my friends won't believe that you came.

From,
Billie

PS If you don't believe me, check my mouth.

PPS I will try to sleep with my mouth open,
but if it's closed, could you come
back in a little while?

PPPS Please don't wake my brother
because he is teething.

Billie tucks the note
under her pillow.
Then her mom gives
her a good-night kiss.

The next morning, when
Billie wakes up, she sits
up slowly. Her knees and
hands still ache and her
chin feels sore. Billie feels
for her wobbly tooth. Oh,
that's right – it's gone!

Billie suddenly
remembers. The Tooth
Fairy! Did she come?
Billie lifts up her pillow.
There, lying on her bed,
is a shiny gold coin.

"Mom, Dad!" Billie yells. She runs to find her parents. Billie's dad is already awake. He has Noah in his arms.

"Shhh…" he says. "Your mom is still sleeping. What is it, Billie?"

"The Tooth Fairy came!" Billie whispers excitedly.

"She must have read my note because she left me money!"

"Well, there you are," says Billie's dad, smiling. "That's great, Billie! It looks like the Tooth Fairy had a busy night. Look!"

Billie's dad gently opens Noah's mouth.

Billie peers inside. And there, on his bottom gum, is a shiny white tooth, as small as a grain of rice.

Billie B. Brown
The Bad Butterfly
By Sally Rippin

Billie B. Brown
The Soccer Star
By Sally Rippin

Billie B. Brown
The Midnight Feast
By Sally Rippin

Billie B. Brown
The Second-best Friend
By Sally Rippin

Billie B. Brown
The Extra-special Helper
By Sally Rippin

Billie B. Brown
The Beautiful Haircut
By Sally Rippin

Billie B. Brown
The Big Sister
By Sally Rippin

Billie B. Brown
The Spotty Vacation
By Sally Rippin

Billie B. Brown
The Birthday Mix-up
By Sally Rippin

Billie B. Brown
The Secret Message
By Sally Rippin

Billie B. Brown
The Little Lie
By Sally Rippin

Billie B. Brown
The Best Project
By Sally Rippin

Billie B. Brown
The Deep End
By Sally Rippin

Billie B. Brown
The Copycat Kid
By Sally Rippin

Billie B. Brown
The Night Fright
By Sally Rippin

Billie B. Brown
The Missing Tooth
By Sally Rippin

Billie B. Brown
The Bully Buster
By Sally Rippin

Billie B. Brown & Hey Jack!
The Book Buddies
By Sally Rippin

Collect them all!
Including a new title starring both Jack AND Bill